"**Did Steve do something to make it look as** if Ti messed up?" Timothy asked.

"Maybe he hid the letter on purpose . . ." added Sarah-Jane.

"*Why* does he want to get you in trouble?" Timothy asked Titus. Suddenly he whispered, "Speaking of Steve—there he is! Duck!"

Can the T.C.D.C. solve *this* mystery?

THE MYSTERY OF THE

SILVER DOLPHIN

Elspeth Campbell Murphy
Illustrated by Chris Wold Dyrud

Chariot Books

x

David C. Cook Publishing Co.

A Wise Owl Book
Published by Chariot Books,
an imprint of David C. Cook Publishing Co.
David C. Cook Publishing Co., Elgin, Illinois 60120
David C. Cook Publishing Co., Weston, Ontario

The Mystery of the Silver Dolphin
© 1988 by Elspeth Campbell Murphy for text and Chris Wold
Dyrud for illustrations

Cover design by Chris Patchel
First Printing, 1988
Printed in the United States of America
93 92 91 90 89 88 5 4 3 2

Library of Congress Cataloging-in-Publication Data

Murphy, Elspeth Campbell.
  The mystery of the Silver Dolphin.

  (Ten commandments mysteries)
  "A Wise owl book."
  Summary: Titus and his two cousins set out to prove his
innocence in the disappearance of a small silver dolphin and
experience the meaning of the commandment, "You shall not give
false testimony."
  [1. Ten commandments—Fiction. 2. Cousins—Fiction. 3.
Mystery and detective stories] I. Dyrud, Chris Wold, ill. II. Title.
III. Series: Murphy, Elspeth Campbell. Ten commandments
mysteries.
PZ7.M95316Myi   1988   [Fic]   87-24925
ISBN 1-55513-515-3

"You shall not give false testimony."

Exodus 20:16 (NIV)

CONTENTS

1
WAITING

Titus McKay loved dolphins.

He loved living in an apartment building called *The Dolphin Towers*.

Titus sat in the lobby of his building and waited impatiently for his cousins Timothy Dawson and Sarah-Jane Cooper to arrive.

It was always hard to wait when his cousins were coming for a visit. But today was especially hard, because Titus had something important to tell them.

To make the waiting go faster, Titus leaned back in the fancy carved chair and looked up. All around the top of the lobby there was a mural painted right on the wall.

Titus had studied the picture hundreds of times before. But he never got tired of looking at it.

The mural showed a deep, blue ocean. And leaping and diving through the waves there were dolphins.

Titus loved the way dolphins always seemed to be smiling or laughing. He knew they were friendly and smart and that sometimes they even let people swim with them. Titus wished he could jump into the picture and go swimming with the dolphins. He wished they would scoop him up and carry him splashing and laughing through the waves.

Titus's friend, Professor Hartman, said that

God must have had fun making dolphins.

She told Titus that the reason she picked their building to live in was because of the name—*Dolphin Towers*.

Professor Hartman taught with Titus's father at the university. But she wasn't teaching any summer classes this year. Instead, she was taking time off to write and illustrate a picture book about dolphins.

Thinking about the Professor reminded Titus of his exciting news.

And that was *perfect timing*—because just then Titus heard the whirring of the revolving door and saw his cousins whizzing past.

Sarah-Jane's father let them go around a couple more times before he said, "Enough, enough! You'll make yourselves sick."

(Titus was used to revolving doors, because he went through them every day. So he didn't think they were that much fun.)

At last Timothy and Sarah-Jane tumbled into the lobby, laughing and dizzy.

"Doorman!" they said to Titus. "Call me a cab!"

"All right!" answered Titus. "You're a cab!"

That was an old city-joke Titus's father had taught them once. And now the cousins said it every time Sarah-Jane visited from the country and Timothy visited from the suburbs.

Uncle Art (Sarah-Jane's dad) was just dropping

the kids off. So he took the bags on upstairs and went to say hello to Titus's parents.

But the cousins hung around the lobby, because Timothy and Sarah-Jane always liked to look at the dolphin mural, too.

"OK!" said Titus, as they rode up on the elevator. "Now for my big news!"

"What big news?" asked Timothy. He was opening and closing his mouth like a fish, because the elevator made his ears pop.

"I have a job!" said Titus proudly.

His cousins looked at him in surprise.

"How can you have a job?" asked Sarah-Jane. "You're just a kid."

"I know," said Titus. "But this is the kind of job a kid can do—except usually only older kids get the chance. But Professor Hartman is trying me out—to see if I can do it."

The elevator reached the nineteenth floor, where Titus lived. But they decided to ride back down to the lobby. Then they would ride back up again.

"So what's the job?" asked Timothy. "Is it detective work?"

(The three cousins *loved* mysteries, and they had even solved some cases together.)

"It's not as good as detective work," said Titus. "But it's *almost* as good. That's because I get to be around dolphins."

"WHAT?!" cried Timothy and Sarah-Jane together.

"No, no, no," said Titus hurriedly. "What I *mean* is, Professor Hartman has the most EXcellent collection of little *statues*. They're all sea animals—like whales and seals and especially *dolphins*. And I get to see them every day. That's because Professor Hartman is super-busy doing a book about dolphins. And she hired me to be her gofer."

"WHAT?!" cried Timothy and Sarah-Jane again.

"You *know*," said Titus. "It's like when she needs something in the neighborhood. I *go for* it. That's why I'm called a '*go-for*.' Get it? *Gofer*?"

"Oh, *now* I do!" cried Sarah-Jane. "At first I thought you meant *gopher*—like the little animal."

"Me, too," said Timothy. "I thought you had

to dress up like a chipmunk or something!''

The idea of Titus dressed up like a chipmunk made them laugh so hard that they fell down.

And riding the elevator sitting down felt so weird, they laughed even harder.

They were laughing so hard they didn't notice that the elevator had reached the lobby. They didn't notice until the doors opened and a crabby-looking older boy got on.

3
A BOY NAMED STEVE

Timothy, Titus, and Sarah-Jane scrambled to their feet.

The older boy gave them a disgusted look and said, "Oh, Titus. You are such a little goof-off!"

"I am not!" said Titus. He boldly reached across the older boy and pushed the button for his own floor.

"Yes, you are," said the older boy. "You are *so dumb*—you don't even know how to ride the elevator! I don't know *why* my aunt hired you to help her. You're too dumb—and too little—to do the job."

"I am not!" said Titus.

"Look, McKay," the older boy went on. "Why don't you just *quit* this gofer job before you *really* mess up?"

"No way, Steve!" said Titus. "I'm not going
to mess up."

"You already have," said Steve. "My aunt
wanted you just now, but I told her you were out
playing."

Titus turned red and said, "That's not true! I
had to wait down in the lobby for my cousins. I
told Professor Hartman that they were coming
today."

Steve looked at Timothy and Sarah-Jane and
rolled his eyes. "*More* babies!" Then he added
in a gooey kind of voice, "Why don't you three

17

little dears just run along and take your naps now?''

Before they could answer him, Steve got out on his floor and the elevator doors closed shut behind him.

"*What . . . is . . . his . . . PROB-LEM?*" exclaimed Sarah-Jane.

They rode up four more floors and walked down the hall to Titus's apartment.

Titus shrugged, "Who knows? Steve is staying with Professor Hartman so he can go to 'enrichment classes' at the university school this summer. His parents are on a trip to Europe. I think Steve is mad that he didn't get to go. And I heard him complaining to some other guy that he doesn't think he gets enough allowance."

Timothy said, "So why didn't he take the gofer job himself and *earn* some extra money?"

"I think he has too much homework," said Titus. "My dad says those enrichment classes are *really hard.*"

"Then why does Steve care if *you* have the gofer job?" asked Sarah-Jane.

"Yeah," said Timothy. "It sure sounds like he

wants you to quit.''

Titus frowned thoughtfully. "I don't know why Steve doesn't want me around.''

"Doesn't it bother you when he calls you dumb?'' asked Timothy.

"Sure it does,'' said Titus. "But my dad says that if somebody calls you dumb, it's because that person is secretly afraid he might be really dumb himself.''

"Ti, you're not the least bit dumb!'' said Sarah-Jane.

Titus grinned. "Thanks, S-J! I needed that. So—I'm just going to ignore Steve. And I'm going to be the best gofer Professor Hartman ever saw!''

4
MESS-UP

Whenever Timothy and Sarah-Jane visited the McKays' apartment, they liked to go out on the balcony and look down until they made themselves woozy.

Usually Titus did this with them. But today he thought he'd better run downstairs and see if Steve was right about the professor wanting him for something.

When Titus came back a little while later, his cousins looked at him in alarm.

"Ti! What's the matter?" asked Timothy.

"You look like something's really bothering you," said Sarah-Jane.

Titus sighed and leaned his head in his hands. "I messed up!"

"What? How?" asked his cousins.

Titus shook his head in a puzzled way. "I don't know. It was the funniest thing. Professor Hartman told me that she had put some important letters on the table by the door. So I took them straight down to the lobby to mail them. And it worked out really well, because I caught up with the mailman just as he was filling up his sack."

"Sounds to *me* like you did a good job," said Timothy.

Titus sighed. "That's what *I* thought, Tim. But when I got back upstairs, the professor and I found one of the important letters on the floor in the hallway outside her door."

"How did it get there?" asked Sarah-Jane.

"I guess I must have dropped it," said Titus miserably. "But I don't know how that could have happened. I tried to be extra careful. I tried to check everything."

"Was the professor mad at you?" asked Timothy.

"No," said Titus. "But I think she's worried that I might be too young to be a good gofer."

"She didn't fire you, did she?" asked Sarah-Jane anxiously.

Titus brightened up a little. "No, she didn't! As a matter of fact, she said it would be all right if I took the letter to the post office. That way, it will still go out in the next pickup. And she asked me to get some index cards at the office supply store, too. That means she still thinks I'm a good gofer. I just hope I don't mess up again!"

"Listen, Ti!" said Timothy excitedly. "How would it be if you had an *assistant gofer*? You know—to double-check stuff—like making sure no envelopes get dropped."

"Yes, Ti!" cried Sarah-Jane as she caught on to what Timothy meant. "How would it be if you had *another* assistant gofer—to *triple*-check stuff?"

"You mean—you guys?" said Titus. "Hey, yeah! That would be great!"

So Titus told his mom where they were going.

Then the three cousins went off to do the gofer work together.

5
FALSE TESTIMONY

At the post office, Titus checked to make sure he was putting the letter in the right slot.

Then Timothy double-checked.

And Sarah-Jane triple-checked.

Titus said, "I still don't understand how I dropped that letter in the hallway. Why didn't I feel it fall? Why didn't I notice it on the dark carpet?"

Neither Timothy nor Sarah-Jane had an answer for that.

The office supply store was right next door to the post office.

They found the index cards without any trouble. And when they paid for them, Titus remembered to ask for a receipt. (Professor Hartman had told him she needed receipts for taxes.)

"The gofer job is working out really well, Ti!" said Sarah-Jane as they started back. "I don't know why Steve says it's too hard for you."

"Steve," said Timothy slowly. "I wonder . . ."

"Wonder what?" asked his cousins.

"I wonder if *Steve* did something with the letter to make it *look* as if Ti messed up?"

"It's possible," said Titus. "Professor Hartman left the letters on the front table. Steve could have taken one. Maybe he hid it on purpose until I went down to the lobby. Then maybe he put the letter in the outside hallway—to make it *look* like I dropped it."

"What a terrible thing to do!" cried Sarah-Jane. "It's—it's like he was telling a lie about you to get you in trouble. One of the Ten Commandments says not to do that. It says, '*You shall not give false testimony*.'"

"Yeah," said Titus. "Like when Steve told the professor I was off playing when I *wasn't*!"

"But, why?" asked Timothy. "Why does Steve want to get you in trouble?"

"To get rid of me, I guess," said Titus.

But that still didn't answer the question—*why*?
Suddenly Timothy whispered, "Speaking of
Steve—there he is! Duck!"

6

A JUNKY LITTLE STORE

The three cousins dove into a nearby doorway. They saw Steve come out of a junky little store. He walked right by on the other side of the street without even seeing them.

"What kind of store is that?" asked Sarah-Jane.

"I'm not sure," said Titus. "Let's take a closer look."

A sign in the window said: *SWAP SHOP—WE BUY AND SELL.*

The cousins opened the door and stepped inside. When they did that, a little bell over the door jangled.

There was no one in the store, and the cousins quickly looked around. They saw piles and piles of all kinds of stuff. Some of it looked interest-

ing. But a lot of it looked like just plain junk.

Just then an old man came out of the back room in answer to the bell.

"Help you?" he asked suspiciously.

Timothy could usually speak up, even when other kids felt too shy. He said, "Uh—we were just wondering—what does that sign in the window mean? Like, if I had something to sell, could I bring it here? And—and then—would you buy it from me and sell it to somebody else?"

"That's how it works," said the man. "But aren't you kind of young to be selling anything?

I'm not sure I need any old toys.''

"Oh! Oh, no! We don't have anything to sell,''
explained Timothy quickly. "We were just wondering. That's all.''

And the three of them turned and hurried out of
the funny little shop.

"What a weird place,'' said Timothy.

"The question is,'' said Titus, "what was
Steve doing there?''

7
TOO MUCH WORK?

"It wasn't all junky stuff," said Sarah-Jane thoughtfully. "In fact, I saw this really neat little dolphin. It was silver, with pretty blue eyes. Maybe the professor would like to buy it for her collection."

"Maybe," said Titus. "But I think she already has one like that."

"Speaking of Steve," said Sarah-Jane. "I hope we don't run into him back at the professor's apartment when we take her the index cards."

"Don't worry," said Titus. "Steve always pretends to be nice when the professor is around."

Titus was right about that.

When Steve opened the door and saw the three of them, he scowled.

But just then the professor came out of her study. So Steve tried hard to sound nice when he said, "Come in, Titus! And these must be your cousins!" (He acted like he had never seen Timothy and Sarah-Jane before.)

Fortunately, the professor wasn't at all like her nephew. Steve was being fake-nice. But the professor was true-nice. And the cousins could tell the difference.

"Thanks for getting the index cards—and the receipt," she said. "And I have another errand. Could you return a book to the library for me? I just remembered—it's due today."

Before Titus could even say, "Sure," Steve jumped up and said, as if he were really concerned, "Aunt Carolyn! Titus is just a little kid! If you give him so much work, you'll wear him out, and he'll quit."

Professor Hartman frowned anxiously. "Is that true, Titus? Am I giving you too much work? Or can you handle it?"

"I can handle it!" said Titus. He felt like sticking his tongue out at Steve, but he knew that would look babyish.

Professor Hartman said, "Well, just be sure to tell me if being a gofer gets too hard. Now, let's find that library book."

Professor Hartman led the three cousins into her study.

Timothy and Sarah-Jane, of course, had never been there before. They were dying to see the collection of sea animals Titus had told them about.

The display shelves were filled with whales and seals and walruses—but mostly dolphins.

The statues were made out of wood or china or

ivory or metal or glass.

Titus asked, "Professor Hartman, did you move some of them around?"

The professor looked at him with a puzzled smile. "No, I don't think so, Titus. Why do you ask?"

Titus said, "Because it looks like there's more space on the shelves than there was when I dusted them yesterday. You didn't lose any statues, did you?"

Professor Hartman shook her head. "I don't see how that could have happened. But I'm afraid I've even lost track of how many I have."

"I counted fifteen yesterday," said Titus.

Quickly the cousins and Professor Hartman counted the statues.

Fourteen.

8
MISSING

"Which one is missing?" asked Sarah-Jane.

The professor and Titus looked at each other, trying to remember. But there were so many statues, they couldn't tell.

Then the professor said, "You know, Titus. I'm not sure *any* of them is missing. I mean, there's no empty spot on the shelf. Perhaps there were only fourteen statues to begin with. Perhaps you miscounted yesterday. The shelves might look different now, because you moved the statues around a bit when you dusted."

Sarah-Jane heaved a sigh of relief and agreed with the professor. Timothy thought it made sense, too.

"Then that must be what happened," said Titus.

But he wasn't really sure. He felt kind of funny about it. Of course, he didn't want any sea animal statue to be lost. But he didn't like to think he had counted wrong, either.

Titus promised himself that he would try to figure out which one was missing—and find it.

Titus said, "Professor Hartman? If it turns out that you really did lose part of your collection, you can call on the T.C.D.C."

"That's good," said the professor. "But what's a 'teesy-deesy'?"

"It's letters," explained Timothy eagerly. "Capital T.

Capital C.

Capital D.

Capital C.

It stands for the Three Cousins Detective Club."

"I'm glad to hear about that," said the professor. "But I do hope I didn't lose any!"

"I hope you didn't lose any, either!" cried Sarah-Jane. "I *love* your collection!"

"Thank you," said the professor. "Do you have any collections?"

"I collect dolls," said Sarah-Jane.

34

"I collect buttons," said Timothy.

"I collect comic books," said Titus. "But I would like to collect dolphins, too."

Professor Hartman showed the cousins some sketches for her picture book.

"Wow!" said Sarah-Jane. "You're a good artist!"

"Thank you," said the professor. "An artist always likes to hear that people enjoy her work."

Titus told his cousins, "Professor Hartman always says that God is the best Artist of all."

"I like that idea!" said Timothy.

"Yes," said Professor Hartman. "Just think of all the colors and shapes God put in His world! And He likes to hear that people enjoy His work."

Thinking about the graceful shapes of the dolphins reminded Titus of the professor's collection. He closed his eyes tight and tried to picture which one might be missing. He almost had it! But not quite.

Then Titus remembered about returning the library book.

"Oh, yes!" said the professor when he reminded her. "What would I do without you, Titus?"

Timothy and Sarah-Jane looked at Titus and grinned. It was clear the professor thought he was a *great* gofer. There was nothing to worry about.

On the way out of the building they stopped to look at the dolphin mural in the lobby.

"You know what?" said Sarah-Jane, as she pointed to a little dolphin. "If you look real hard, you can tell that this dolphin has blue eyes, too. Just like the one I saw in the Swap Shop. Dolphins don't *really* have blue eyes, do they? It just looks that way in the picture, right, Ti?"

Titus stopped dead in his tracks. "Sapphires!"

he said. "Sapphires!"

"WHAT?" cried Timothy and Sarah-Jane.

They tried hard to understand what Titus was getting at. Timothy said, "Sapphires are some kind of jewels, right?"

"*Blue* jewels," said Titus urgently. "Sapphires are *blue*. I just realized which statue is missing. It's a little silver one with sapphire eyes! We have to go back to the Swap Shop. I have to find out if the dolphin Sarah-Jane saw there is the same one that's missing from the professor's collection!"

The cousins practically flew out of the revolving door.

They ran all the way to the library which—fortunately—was on the way.

Titus dashed up the steps, dropped the book off, and dashed back outside again. Timothy and Sarah-Jane were bouncing up and down with impatience.

The cousins set the little bell jangling wildly as they burst through the Swap Shop door.

Sarah-Jane led the boys straight to the little silver dolphin with the blue sapphire eyes. It was

beautiful. It seemed to be leaping for joy at being a dolphin.

"That's it!" panted Titus.

"Are you sure?" asked Timothy.

"Positive!"

The old man hurried out from the back room. "What's going on?" he demanded. "What are you three doing back here?"

Timothy said, "That little dolphin belongs to a friend of ours!"

"No, it doesn't, Sonny," said the man. "It belongs to me now—until someone else buys it."

38

"A boy called Steve sold it to you, didn't he?" asked Titus.

"That's not for me to say," replied the man.

But he didn't have to say anything. The cousins already *knew*. Steve had stolen the professor's dolphin and sold it to the Swap Shop man. And there was nothing they could do about it—except tell the professor.

When they came out of the Swap Shop, who should they see about a block ahead of them—but Steve.

And Steve saw them.

For a split second, they all stood staring.

"He saw us coming out of the Swap Shop," said Titus. "He knows that we figured out what he did."

Suddenly Steve turned and ran.

"After him!" cried Timothy. "He's going back to the apartment building! And if I know Steve, he's going to make up some lie to tell his aunt. We have to tell her the *truth*!"

The three cousins took off after Steve. But he had a big head start. And he could run faster than they could.

When they got to the lobby, Steve was nowhere to be seen.

It seemed like it took *forever* for the elevator to get there. "Oh, come on, come on, come on, *come on*!'' the cousins muttered under their breath. And then it seemed like the elevator stopped on *every floor*. "Oh, come on, come on, come on, *come on*!"

Finally it reached fifteen, where the professor lived. The cousins tumbled out and raced down the hall. Titus knocked on the door.

"Titus!" said the professor in surprise when she opened the door. "I was just about to call you. There's something we need to talk about. Come in."

She wasn't smiling.

As soon as the cousins stepped into the living room, they saw Steve. He gave them a sad little smile and shook his head.

"I'm sorry, Titus," he said. "But I had to tell my aunt what you did."

"WHAT?!" yelled Timothy and Sarah-Jane.

Titus turned to the professor. He swallowed hard and said in a small voice, "What did Steve tell you?"

Professor Hartman took a deep breath. "He says he saw you put one of the statues in your pocket yesterday, Titus. He says he thought I had told you that you could borrow it. But then this afternoon—he saw you and your cousins coming out of the Swap Shop. Steve thinks you stole the statue and sold it.''

The cousins could hardly believe their ears.

Sarah-Jane stamped her foot. (She only did that when she was *very* upset.) She turned bright red and yelled at Steve, ''You're doing it again! You're giving *false testimony*, like the Bible says not to. You're making up lies about my cousin just to get him in trouble.''

''Yeah, Steve!'' yelled Timothy. ''Ti didn't take the statue and sell it—*you* did!''

Titus said, ''*I'm* not the one who took the statue! *I'm* the one who noticed it was gone! Steve, *you* took the statue and moved the other ones so there wouldn't be an empty spot.''

''I did not!'' Steve yelled. ''I never touched the statue collection. I never even *looked* at them!''

The professor pressed her fingers against her eyebrows as if she were getting a headache. She looked very unhappy and confused.

Suddenly Titus had an idea. He didn't think Steve could pass up a chance to say what a dumb little kid he was. At least he hoped not. He said to Professor Hartman, "Which statue did Steve say I took? Was it the little silver dolphin—the one with the ruby eyes?"

"Oh, Titus!" said Steve in a big-kid, know-it-all voice. "Don't you know anything? Rubies are *red—not blue*! That dolphin's eyes are *sapphires*!" Steve stopped and clapped his hand over his mouth.

The professor stared at her nephew. "How do *you* know that, Steve? Unless *you* took the dolphin yourself?"

Steve glared at Titus. "You tricked me!"

Titus shrugged. "Maybe. But at least I didn't make up lies about you. At least I wasn't trying to get rid of you!"

Professor Hartman stood over Steve with her hands on her hips. "Is this true? Were you trying to get me to fire Titus?"

Steve nodded miserably.

"*Why*?"

Steve stared at the floor. "Because I was going to take some statues and sell them—one at a time. I figured you were so busy writing your book that

you wouldn't notice.

"But you hired Titus to be your gofer. And he notices *everything*. I keep saying how dumb he is. But he's really one of the smartest little kids I ever saw. When he's older he'll probably go to enrichment classes at the university school. But I hate going—I'm too dumb."

Professor Hartman put her arm around her nephew. "No, you're not! But I hadn't realized how unhappy you've been, Steve. That's no excuse for what you did, though. I see that you and I need to have a *long talk*!"

Steve looked up. "But first, Aunt Carolyn, I want to go back to the Swap Shop and buy back your dolphin, OK? I still have the money."

His aunt said, "Yes, we'll do that together. But *first* you must apologize to Titus."

Steve said he was sorry, and Titus said it was OK.

"And I'm sorry, too, Titus," said Professor Hartman. "How could I have doubted you? You're the best gofer I ever saw!"

On the way back upstairs, Titus remembered another exciting thing he had to tell his cousins.

"Guess what! For supper tonight, Mom and Dad and I are taking you out to our favorite pizza place!"

"Hooray!" cried Sarah-Jane. "I *love* pizza!"

"Pizza, huh?" said Timothy. "I could really *go fer* that!"

The End

THE TEN COMMANDMENTS MYSTERIES

When Timothy, Titus, and Sarah-Jane, the three cousins, get together the most ordinary events turn into mysteries. So they've formed the T.C.D.C. (That's the Three Cousins Detective Club.)

And while the three cousins are solving mysteries, they're also learning about the Ten Commandments and living God's way.

You'll want to solve all ten mysteries along with Sarah-Jane, Ti, and Tim:

The Mystery of the Laughing Cat—"You shall not steal." *Someone stole rare coins. Can the cousins find the thief?*

The Mystery of the Messed-up Wedding—"You shall not commit adultery." *Can the cousins find the missing wedding ring?*

The Mystery of the Gravestone Riddle—"You shall not murder." *Can the cousins solve a 100-year-old murder case?*

The Mystery of the Carousel Horse—"You shall not covet." *Why does the stranger want an old, wooden horse?*

The Mystery of the Vanishing Present—"Remember the Sabbath day and keep it holy." *Can the cousins figure out who has Grandpa's missing birthday gift?*

The Mystery of the Silver Dolphin—"You shall not give false testimony." *Who's telling the truth—and who's lying?*

The Mystery of the Tattletale Parrot—"You shall not misuse the name of the Lord your God." *What will the beautiful green parrot say next?*

The Mystery of the Second Map—"You shall have no other gods before me." *Can the cousins discover who dropped the strange map?*

The Mystery of the Double Trouble—"Honor your father and your mother." *How could Timothy be in two places at once?*

The Mystery of the Silent Idol—"You shall not make for yourself an idol." *If the idol could speak, what would it tell the cousins?*

Available at your local Christian bookstore.

David C. Cook Publishing Co., Elgin, IL 60120

SHOELACES AND BRUSSELS SPROUTS

One little lie, but BIG trouble!

When Alex lies to her mom about losing her shoelaces, it doesn't seem like a big deal. But how do you replace special baseball laces when you don't have any money and you're not allowed to go to the store alone? A big softball game is coming up, and Alex knows the coach won't let her pitch in shoes without laces—or in cowboy boots!

Every kid gets into the predicaments that Alex does—ones that start out small and mushroom. Readers will learn from Alex's mistakes and understand that they have the same sources of help that she turns to: A God who loves them and wants to help them, and parents who understand.

Other books in the Alex Series . . .

2 *French Fry Forgiveness*—Sometimes making friends is harder than making enemies.

3 *Hot Chocolate Friendship*—Is winning first place as important to Alex as being a friend?

4 *Peanut Butter and Jelly Secrets*—Obeying her parents (even in little things) beats the awful results of disobeying.

Available at your local Christian bookstore.

David C. Cook Publishing Co.
850 N. Grove Ave.
Elgin, IL 60120

Chariot Books